She knew every bird in the woods
behind her house.

"Hello,
Mr Blackbird!"

"Hello,
Mr Woodpecker!"

"Morning,
Mrs Sparrow!"

But, one day, Martha spotted someone new.

She'd never seen a bird
like this before. It was
really funny-looking.

And big, too.
The biggest bird that
Martha had ever seen.

"Hello,
Mr Whoever-You-Are!"
she said.

The bird was a little shy at first,
but it soon took a shine to her.

It was very funny and friendly.

"But I still don't know what you are,"
said Martha. "I think I'll have to
look you up in my books."

It was a dodo – and it was supposed to be *extinct*!

Once there had been thousands of them, then they all disappeared. People had hunted them and eaten them for dinner.

No one had seen a dodo for hundreds of years.

DODO
(Raphus cucullatus)
EXTINCT

This was also the fate of the Moa bird of New Zealand. Many species of Moa once roamed the forests of New Zealand, some of them growing to more than three metres in height.

However, by the mid-1400s the Moa were all gone. They had been hunted to extinction when the Maori people arrived in New Zealand from Polynesia.

Other FLIGHTLESS BIRDS
MOA

Dodos are not the only flightless birds to have become extinct after the arrival of human settlers.

The dodo has become a powerful symbol of endangered and extinct species.

An extinct flightless bird unique to Mauritius, an island to the southeast of the African continent.

Much about the dodo bird is unknown.

They were believed to have lived in wooded areas of the coast of the island. They grew to one metre in height, laid one egg at a time and had a diet consisting mainly of soft fruits and seeds.

The first recorded mention of the dodo was by Dutch sailors in 1598. It is thought that the hungry sailors hunted the bird to extinction not long after.

The fact that dodos were unable to fly, and had never been hunted before, made them particularly easy to catch.

The last sighting of a dodo was in 1662.

Records suggest that, before then, many dodos were transported to Europe, Asia and elsewhere. It is not known whether any of the birds survived these long journeys.

Extinction of the dodo was not formally accepted until the 19th century.

Mauritius 1648

"Poor things," thought Martha.
"Well, they're not going to eat *my* dodo."
And she decided to keep him a secret.

That summer, Martha learned a lot about dodos.

They were *terrible* at playing snap.

They *really* couldn't fly.

They *loved* doughnuts.

And they made the best friends *ever*.

All this time, Martha kept the dodo a secret.

Then, one afternoon . . .

. . . the secret just slipped out.

"Where are you off to with all those doughnuts?" asked the postman. "They're for my dodo," said Martha. "Dodos *love* doughnuts."

Oh, no!

What had she said? Now the postman might tell everyone in town. What would happen to Mr Dodo if people found him? She had to warn him – fast!

"Quick!" said Martha.
"You've got to hide!"

But the dodo just wanted doughnuts.

"I can't visit you any more," said Martha.
"They might see me."

But he didn't seem to understand.

"Goodbye, Mr Dodo," she sighed.
"Let's hope the postman doesn't tell anyone about you."

Unfortunately, he did.

The next day, a huge crowd gathered outside Martha's door. They were from the television, the newspapers, and the zoo. They were all shouting:

"Where's the dodo, Martha?"

What could Martha say?

So she said . . .

"He's right here!

"Can't you see him? Hello, Mr Dodo!
Would you like a doughnut?"

"He's an *imaginary* dodo?" said the postman.
"But, of course," said Martha. "Dodos are extinct.
Everyone knows that!"

The crowd were very grumpy as they packed up and left.
But would it ever be safe for Martha to go and see the dodo again?
What if somebody spotted her?

As summer turned
to autumn . . .

. . . and autumn to winter,
Martha thought about
her friend.

She began to wonder whether she really had imagined him after all.

When spring came, she decided she had to go back and see.
She took some doughnuts with her, just in case.

She looked in all their
favourite places,

but she couldn't see him.

Then she held up her bag
of doughnuts, and shook it.
"Doughnuts, Mr Dodo!"
she whispered.

There was a rustle in
the bushes behind her . . .

. . . and there he was!
"Mr Dodo!" cried Martha.
"You're safe!"

And it seemed he'd been keeping
a secret of his own. There was
another dodo with him . . .

. . . and an egg!

BIRD SPOTTING
know your birds

1.
2.
3.
4.
5.
6.
7.

Other:

NAME: Martha

1. blackbird ☑
2. gull ☑
3. pigeon ☑
4. oystercatcher ☑
5. sparrow ☑
6. magpie ☑
7. woodpecker ☑

Other: dodo

For Mum and Dad, just because

First published in the UK in 2016 by Alison Green Books, an imprint of Scholastic Children's Books
Euston House, 24 Eversholt Street, London, NW1 1DB. A division of Scholastic Ltd. www.scholastic.co.uk
London – New York – Toronto – Sydney – Auckland – Mexico City – New Delhi – Hong Kong
Copyright © 2016 Nicholas John Frith. All rights reserved. Moral rights asserted.
HB ISBN: 978 1 407146 42 3 • PB ISBN: 978 1 407146 43 0
Printed in Malaysia
1 3 5 7 9 8 6 4 2
Papers used by Scholastic Children's Books are made from wood grown in sustainable forests.